THE LOST VALLEY OF ISKANDER

BY

ROBERT E. HOWARD

British Library Cataloguing-in-Publication Data
A catalogue record for this book is available from the
British Library

Contents

Robert E. Howard

Robert Ervin Howard was born in Peaster, Texas in 1906. During his youth, his family moved between a variety of Texan boomtowns, and Howard – a bookish and somewhat introverted child – was steeped in the violent myths and legends of the Old South. Although he loved reading and learning, Howard developed a distinctly Texan, hardboiled outlook on the world. He became a passionate fan of boxing, taking it up at an amateur level, and from the age of nine began to write adventure tales of semi-historical bloodshed. In 1919, when Howard was thirteen, his family moved to the Central Texas hamlet of Cross Plains, where he would stay for the rest of his life.

At fifteen Howard began to read the pulp magazines of the day, and to write more seriously. The December 1922 issue of his high school newspaper featured two of his stories, 'Golden Hope Christmas' and 'West is West'. In 1924 he sold his first piece – a short caveman tale titled 'Spear and Fang' – for $16 to the not-yet-famous *Weird Tales* magazine. He published with the magazine regularly over the next few years. 1929 was a breakout year for Howard, in that the 23-year-old writer began to sell to other magazines, such as *Ghost Stories* and *Argosy,* both of whom had previously sent him hundreds of rejection slips. In 1930, he began a correspondence with weird fiction master H. P. Lovecraft which ran up to his death six years later, and is regarded as one of the great correspondence cycles in all of fantasy literature.

It was partly due to Lovecraft's encouragement that Howard created his most famous character, Conan the Cimmerian. Conan – a barbarian-turned-King during the Hyborian Age, a mythical period of some 12,000 years ago – featured in seventeen *Weird Tales* stories between 1933 and 1936, and is now regarded as having spawned the 'sword and sorcery' genre, making Howard's influence on fantasy literature comparable to that of J. R. R. Tolkien's. The Conan stories have since been adapted many times, most famously in the series of films starring Arnold Schwarzenegger.

Howard was enjoying an all-time high in sales by the beginning of 1936, but he was also deeply upset by the ill health of his mother, who had fallen into a coma. On the morning of June 11, 1936, he asked an attending nurse whether she would ever recover, and the nurse replied negatively. Howard walked to his car, parked outside the family home in Cross Plains, and shot himself. He died eight hours later, aged just thirty.

THE LOST VALLEY OF ISKANDER

IT WAS THE stealthy clink of steel on stone that wakened Gordon. In the dim starlight a shadowy bulk loomed over him and something glinted in the lifted hand. Gordon went into action like a steel spring uncoiling. His left hand checked the descending wrist with its curved knife, and simultaneously he heaved upward and locked his right hand savagely on a hairy throat.

A gurgling gasp was strangled in that throat and Gordon, resisting the other's terrific plunges, hooked a leg about his knee and heaved him over and underneath. There was no sound except the rasp and thud of straining bodies. Gordon fought, as always, in grim silence. No sound came from the straining lips of the man beneath. His right hand writhed in Gordon's grip while his left tore futilely at the wrist whose iron fingers drove deeper and deeper into the throat they grasped. That wrist felt like a mass of woven steel wires to the weakening fingers that clawed at it. Grimly Gordon maintained his position, driving all the power of his compact shoulders and corded arms into his throttling fingers. He knew it was his life or that of the man who had crept up to stab him in the dark. In that unmapped corner of the Afghan mountains all fights were to the death. The tearing fingers relaxed. A convulsive shudder ran through the great body straining beneath the American. It went limp.

I. THE OILED SILK PACKAGE

GORDON SLID OFF the corpse, in the deeper shadow of the great rocks among which he had been sleeping. Instinctively he felt under his arm to see if the precious package for which he had staked his life was still safe. Yes, it was there, that flat bundle of papers wrapped in oiled silk, that meant life or death to thousands. He listened. No sound broke the stillness. About him the slopes with their ledges and boulders rose gaunt and black in the starlight. It was the darkness before the dawn.

But he knew that men moved about him, out there among the rocks. His ears, whetted by years in wild places, caught stealthy sounds—the soft rasp of cloth over stones, the faint shuffle of sandalled feet. He could not see them, and he knew they could not see him, among the clustered boulders he had chosen for his sleeping site.

His left hand groped for his rifle, and he drew his revolver with his right. That short, deadly fight had made no more noise than the silent knifing of a sleeping man might have made. Doubtless his stalkers out yonder were awaiting some signal from the man they had sent in to murder their victim.

Gordon knew who these men were. He knew their leader was the man who had dogged him for hundreds of miles, determined he should not reach India with that silk-wrapped packet. Francis Xavier Gordon was known by repute from Stamboul to the China Sea. The Muhammadans called him El Borak, the Swift, and they feared and respected him. But in Gustav Hunyadi, renegade and international adventurer, Gordon had met his match. And he knew now that Hunyadi, out there in the night, was lurking with his Turkish killers. They had ferreted him out, at last.

Gordon glided out from among the boulders as silently as a great cat. No hillman, born and bred among those crags, could have avoided loose stones more skillfully or picked his way more carefully. He headed southward, because that was the direction in which lay his ultimate goal. Doubtless he was completely surrounded.

His soft native sandals made no noise, and in his dark hillman's garb he was all but invisible. In the pitch-black shadow of an overhanging cliff, he suddenly sensed a human presence ahead of him. A voice hissed, a European tongue framing the Turki words: "Ali! Is that you? Is the dog dead? Why did you not call me?"

Gordon struck savagely in the direction of the voice. His pistol barrel crunched glancingly against a human skull, and a man groaned and crumpled. All about rose a sudden clamor of voices, the rasp of leather on rock. A stentorian voice began shouting, with a note of panic.

Gordon cast stealth to the winds. With a bound he cleared the writhing body before him, and sped off down the slope. Behind him rose a chorus of yells as the men in hiding glimpsed his shadowy figure racing through the starlight. Jets of orange cut the darkness, but the bullets whined high and wide. Gordon's flying shape was sighted but an instant, then the shadowy gulfs of the night swallowed it up. His enemies raved like foiled wolves in their bewildered rage. Once again their prey had slipped like an eel through their fingers and was gone.

So thought Gordon as he raced across the plateau beyond the clustering cliffs. They would be hot after him, with hillmen who could trail a wolf across naked rocks, but with the start he had—. Even with the thought the earth gaped blackly before him. Even his steel-trap quickness could not save him. His grasping hands caught only thin air as he plunged downward, to strike his head with stunning force at the bottom.

When he regained his senses a chill dawn was whitening the sky. He sat up groggily and felt his head, where a large lump was clotted with dried blood. It was only by chance that his neck was not broken. He had fallen into a ravine, and during the precious time he should have employed in flight, he was lying senseless among the rocks at the bottom.

Again he felt for the packet under his native shirt, though he knew it was fastened there securely. Those papers were his death-warrant, which only his skill and wit could prevent being executed. Men had laughed when Francis Xavier Gordon had warned them that the devil's own stew was bubbling in Central Asia, where a satanic adventurer was dreaming of an outlaw empire.

To prove his assertion, Gordon had gone into Turkestan, in guise of a wandering Afghan. Years spent in the Orient had given him the ability to pass himself for a native anywhere. He had secured proof no one could ignore or deny, but he had been recognized at last. He had fled for his life, and for more than his life, then. And Hunyadi, the renegade who plotted the destruction of nations, was hot on his heels. He had followed Gordon across the steppes, through the foothills, and up into the mountains where he had thought at last to throw him off. But he had failed. The Hungarian was a human bloodhound. Wary, too, as shown by his sending his craftiest slayer in to strike a blow in the dark.

Gordon found his rifle and began the climb out of the ravine. Under his left arm was proof that would make certain officials wake up and take steps to prevent the atrocious thing that Gustav Hunyadi planned. The proof was in the form of letters to various Central Asian chiefs, signed and sealed with the Hungarian's own hand. They revealed his whole plot to embroil Central Asia in a religious war and send howling hordes of fanatics against the Indian border. It was a plan for plundering on a staggering scale. That package must reach Fort Ali Masjid! With all his iron will Francis Xavier Gordon was determined it should. With equal resolution Gustav Hunyadi was determined it should not. In the clash of two such indomitable temperaments, kingdoms shake and death reaps a red harvest.

Dirt crumbled and pebbles rattled down as Gordon worked his way up the sloping side of the ravine. But presently he clambered over the edge and cast a quick look about him. He was on a narrow plateau, pitched among giant slopes which rose somberly above it. To the south showed the mouth of a narrow gorge, walled by rocky cliffs. In that direction he hurried.

He had not gone a dozen steps when a rifle cracked behind him. Even as the wind of the bullet fanned his cheek, Gordon dropped flat behind a boulder, a sense of futility tugging at his heart. He could never escape Hunyadi. This chase would end only when one of them was dead. In the increasing light he saw figures moving among the boulders along the slopes of the northwest of the plateau. He had lost his chance of escaping under cover of darkness, and now it looked like a finish fight.

He thrust forward his rifle barrel. Too much to hope that that blind blow in the dark had killed Hunyadi. The man had as many lives as a cat. A bullet splattered on the boulder close to his elbow. He had seen a tongue of flame lick out, marking the spot where the sniper lurked. He watched those rocks, and when a head and part of an arm and shoulder came up with a rifle, Gordon fired. It was a long shot, but the man reared upright and pitched forward across the rock that had sheltered him.

More bullets came, spattering Gordon's refuge. Up on the slopes, where the big boulders poised breathtakingly, he saw his enemies moving like ants, wriggling from ledge to ledge. They were spread out in a wide ragged semi-circle, trying to surround him again. He did not have enough ammunition to stop them. He dared shoot only when fairly certain of scoring a hit. He dared not make a break for the gorge behind him. He would be riddled before he could reach it. It looked like trail's end for him, and while Gordon had faced death too often to fear it greatly, the thought that those papers would never reach their destination filled him with black despair.

A bullet whining off his boulder from a new angle made him crouch lower, seeking the marksman. He glimpsed a white turban, high up on the slope, above the others. From that position the Turk could drop bullets directly into Gordon's covert.

The American could not shift his position, because a dozen other rifles nearer at hand were covering it; and he could not stay where he was. One of those dropping slugs would find him sooner or later. But the Ottoman decided that he saw a still better position, and risked a shift, trusting to the long uphill range. He did not know Gordon as Hunyadi knew him.

The Hungarian, further down the slope, yelled a fierce command, but the Turk was already in motion, headed for another ledge, his garments flapping about him. Gordon's bullet caught him in mid-stride. With a wild cry he staggered, fell headlong and crashed against a poised boulder. He was a heavy man, and the impact of his hurtling body toppled the rock from its unstable base. It rolled down the slope, dislodging others as it came. Dirt rattled in widening streams about it.

Men began recklessly to break cover. Gordon saw Hunyadi spring up and run obliquely across the slope, out of the path of the sliding rocks. The tall supple figure was unmistakable, even in Turkish garb. Gordon fired and missed, as he always seemed to miss the man, and then there was no time to fire again. The whole slope was in motion now, thundering down in a bellowing, grinding torrent of stones and dirt and boulders. The Turks were fleeing after Hunyadi, screaming: "Ya Allah!"

Gordon sprang up and raced for the mouth of the gorge. He did not look back. He heard above the roaring, the awful screams that marked the end of men caught and crushed and ground to bloody shreds under the rushing tons of shale and stone. He dropped his rifle. Every ounce of extra burden counted now. A deafening roar was in his ears as he gained the mouth of the gorge and flung himself about the beetling jut of the cliff. He crouched there, flattened against the wall, and through the gorge mouth roared a welter of dirt and rocks, boulders bouncing and tumbling, rebounding thunderously from the sides and hurtling on down the sloping pass. Yet, it was a only a trickle of the avalanche which was diverted into the gorge. The main bulk of it thundered on down the mountain.

II. THE RESCUE OF BARDYLIS OF ATTALUS

GORDON PULLED AWAY from the cliff that had sheltered him. He stood knee deep in loose dirt and broken stones. A flying splinter of stone had cut his face. The roar of the landslide was followed by an unearthly silence. Looking back on to the plateau, he saw a vast litter of broken earth, shale and rocks. Here and there an arm or a leg protruded, bloody and twisted, to mark where a human victim had been caught by the torrent. Of Hunyadi and the survivors there was no sign.

But Gordon was a fatalist where the satanic Hungarian was concerned. He felt quite sure that Hunyadi had survived, and would be upon his trail again as soon as he could collect his demoralized followers. It was likely that he would recruit the natives of these hills to his service. The man's power among the followers of Islam was little short of marvelous.

So Gordon turned hurriedly down the gorge. Rifle, pack of supplies, all were lost. He had only the garments on his body and the pistol at his hip. Starvation in these barren mountains was a haunting threat, if he escaped being butchered by the wild tribes which inhabited them. There was about one chance in ten thousand of his ever getting out alive. But he had known it was a desperate quest when he started, and long odds had never balked Francis Xavier Gordon, once of El Paso, Texas, and now for years soldier of fortune in the outlands of the world.

The gorge twisted and bent between tortuous walls. The split-off arm of the avalanche had quickly spent its force there, but Gordon still saw the slanting floor littered with boulders which had stumbled down from the higher levels. And suddenly he stopped short, his pistol snapping to a level.

On the ground before him lay a man such as he had never seen in the Afghan mountains or elsewhere. He was young, but tall and strong, clad in short silk breeches, tunic and sandals, and girdled with a broad belt which supported a curved sword.

His hair caught Gordon's attention. Blue eyes, such as the youth had, were not uncommon in the hills. But his hair was yellow, bound to his temples with a band of red cloth, and falling in a square-cut mane nearly to his shoulders. He was clearly no Afghan. Gordon remembered tales he had heard of a tribe living somewhere in these mountains who were neither Afghans nor Muhammadans. Had he stumbled upon a member of that legendary race?

The youth was vainly trying to draw his sword. He was pinned down by a boulder which had evidently caught him as he raced for the shelter of the cliff.

"Slay me and be done with it, you Moslem dog!" he gritted in Pushtu.

"I won't harm you," answered Gordon. "I'm no Moslem. Lie still. I'll help you if I can. I have no quarrel with you."

The heavy stone lay across the youth's leg in such a way that he could not extricate the member.

"Is your leg broken?" Gordon asked.

"I think not. But if you move the stone it will grind it to shreds."

Gordon saw that he spoke the truth. A depression on the under side of the stone had saved the youth's limb, while imprisoning it. If he rolled the boulder either way, it would crush the member.

"I'll have to lift it straight up," he grunted.

"You can never do it," said the youth despairingly. "Ptolemy himself could scarecely lift it, and you are not nearly so big as he."

Gordon did not pause to inquire who Ptolemy might be, nor to explain that strength is not altogether a matter of size alone. His own thews were like masses of knit steel wires.

Yet he was not at all sure that he could lift that boulder, which, while not so large as many which rolled down the gorge, was yet bulky enough to make the task look dubious. Straddling the prisoner's body, he braced his legs wide, spread his arms and gripped the big stone. Putting all his corded sinews and his scientific knowledge of weight-lifting into his effort, he uncoiled his strength in a smooth, mighty expansion of power.

His heels dug into the dirt, the veins in his temples swelled, and unexpected knots of muscles sprang out on his straining arms. But the great stone came up steadily without a jerk or waver, and the man on the ground drew his leg clear and rolled away.

Gordon let the stone fall and stepped back, shaking the perspiration from his face. The other worked his skinned, bruised leg gingerly, then looked up and extended his hand in a curiously unOriental gesture.

"I am Bardylis of Attalus," he said. "My life is yours!"

"Men call me El Borak," answered Gordon, taking his hand. They made a strong contrast: the tall, rangy youth in his strange garb, with his white skin and yellow hair, and the American, shorter, more compactly built, in his tattered Afghan garments, and his sun-darkened skin. Gordon's hair was straight and black as an Indian's, and his eyes were black as his hair.

"I was hunting on the cliffs," said Bardylis. "I heard shots and was going to investigate them, when I heard the roar of the avalanche and the gorge was filled with flying rocks. You are no Pathan, despite your name. Come to my village. You look like a man who is weary and has lost his way."

"Where is your village?"

"Yonder, down the gorge and beyond the cliffs." Bardylis pointed southward. Then, looking over Gordon's shoulder, he cried out. Gordon wheeled. High up on the beetling gorge wall, a turbaned head was poked from behind a ledge. A dark face stared down wildly. Gordon ripped out his pistol with a snarl, but the face vanished and he heard a frantic voice yelling in guttural Turki. Other voices answered, among which the American recognized the strident accents of Gustav Hunyadi. The pack was at his heels again. Undoubtedly they had seen Gordon take refuge in the gorge, and as soon as the boulders ceased tumbling, had traversed the torn slope and followed the cliffs where they would have the advantage of the man below.

But Gordon did not pause to ruminate. Even as the turbaned head vanished, he wheeled with a word to his companion, and darted around the next bend in the canyon. Bardylis followed without question, limping on his bruised leg, but moving with sufficient alacrity. Gordon heard his pursuers shouting on the cliff above and behind him, heard them crashing recklessly through stunted bushes, dislodging pebbles as they ran, heedless of everything except their desire to sight their quarry.

Although the pursuers had one advantage, the fugitives had another. They could follow the slightly slanting floor of the gorge more swiftly than the others could run along the uneven cliffs, with their broken edges and jutting ledges. They had to climb and scramble, and Gordon heard their maledictions growing fainter in the distance behind him. When they emerged from the further mouth of the gorge, they were far in advance of Hunyadi's killers.

But Gordon knew that the respite was brief. He looked about him. The narrow gorge had opened out onto a trail which ran straight along the crest of a cliff that fell away sheer three hundred feet into a deep valley, hemmed in on all sides by gigantic precipices. Gordon looked down and saw a stream winding among dense trees far below, and further on, what seemed to be stone buildings among the groves.

Bardylis pointed to the latter.

"There is my village!" he said excitedly. "If we could get into the valley we would be safe! This trail leads to the pass at the southern end, but it is five miles distant!"

Gordon shook his head. The trail ran straight along the top of the cliff and afforded no cover. "They'll run us down and shoot us like rats at long range, if we keep to this path."

"There is one other way!" cried Bardylis. "Down the cliff, at this very point! It is a secret way, and none but a man of my people has ever followed it, and then only when hard pressed. There are handholds cut into the rock. Can you climb down?"

"I'll try," answered Gordon, sheathing his pistol. To try to go down those towering cliffs looked like suicide, but it was sure death to try to outrun Hunyadi's rifles along the trail. At any minute he expected the Magyar and his men to break cover.

"I will go first and guide you," said Bardylis rapidly, kicking off his sandals and letting himself over the cliff edge. Gordon did likewise and followed him. Clinging to the sharp lip of the precipice, Gordon saw a series of small holes pitting the rock. He began the descent slowly, clinging like a fly to a wall. It was hair-raising work, and the only thing that made it possible at all was the slight convex slant of the hill at that point. Gordon had made many a desperate climb during his career, but never one which put such strain on nerve and thew. Again and again only the grip of a finger stood between him and death. Below him Bardylis toiled downward, guiding and encouraging him, until the youth finally dropped to the earth and stood looking tensely up at the man above him.

Then he shouted, with a note of strident fear in his voice. Gordon, still twenty feet from the bottom, craned his neck upward. High above him he saw a bearded face peering down at him, convulsed with triumph. Deliberately the Turk sighted downward with a pistol, then laid it aside and caught up a heavy stone, leaning far over the edge to aim its downward course. Clinging with toes and nails, Gordon drew and fired upward with the same motion. Then he flattened himself desperately against the cliff and clung on.

The man above screamed and pitched headfirst over the brink. The rock rushed down, striking Gordon a glancing blow on the shoulder, then the writhing body hurtled past and struck with a sickening concussion on the earth below. A voice shouting furiously high above announced the presence of Hunyadi at last, and Gordon slid and tumbled recklessly the remaining distance, and, with Bardylis, ran for the shelter of the trees.

A glance backward and upward showed him Hunyadi crouching on the cliff, leveling a rifle, but the next instant Gordon and Bardylis were out of sight, and Hunyadi, apparently dreading an answering shot from the trees, made a hasty retreat with the four Turks who were the survivors of his party.

III. THE SONS OF ISKANDER

"YOU SAVED MY life when you showed me that path," said Gordon.

Bardylis smiled. "Any man of Attalus could have shown you the path, which we call the Road of the Eagles. But only a hero could have followed it. From what land comes my brother?"

"From the west," answered Gordon; "from the land of America, beyond Frankistan and the sea."

Bardylis shook his head. "I have never heard of it. But come with me. My people are yours henceforth."

As they moved through the trees, Gordon scanned the cliffs in vain for some sign of his enemies. He felt certain that neither Hunyadi, bold as he was, nor any of his companions would try to follow them down "the Road of the Eagles." They were not mountaineers. They were more at home in the saddle than on a hill path. They would seek some other way into the valley. He spoke his thoughts to Bardylis.

"They will find death," answered the youth grimly. "The Pass of the King, at the southern end of the valley, is the only entrance. Men guard it with matchlocks night and day. The only strangers who enter the Valley of Iskander are traders and merchants with pack-mules."

21

Gordon inspected his companion curiously, aware of a certain tantalizing sensation of familiarity he could not place.

"Who are your people?" he asked. "You are not an Afghan. You do not look like a Oriental at all."

"We are the Sons of Iskander," answered Bardylis. "When the great conqueror came through these mountains long ago, he built the city we call Attalus, and left hundreds of his soldiers and their women in it. Iskander marched westward again, and after a long while word came that he was dead and his empire divided. But the people of Iskander abode here, unconquered. Many times we have slaughtered the Afghan dogs who came against us."

Light came to Gordon, illuminating that misplaced familiarity. Iskander—Alexander the Great, who conquered this part of Asia and left colonies behind him. This boy's profile was classic Grecian, such as Gordon had seen in sculptured marble, and the names he spoke were Grecian. Undoubtedly he was the descendant of some Macedonian soldier who had followed the Great Conqueror on his invasion of the East.

To test the matter, he spoke to Bardylis in ancient Greek, one of the many languages, modern and obsolete, he had picked up in his varied career. The youth cried out with pleasure.

"You speak our tongue!" he exclaimed, in the same language. "Not in a thousand years has a stranger come to us with our own speech on his lips. We converse with the Moslems in their own tongue, and they know nothing of ours. Surely, you too, are a Son of Iskander?"

Gordon shook his head, wondering how he could explain his knowledge of the tongue to this youth who knew nothing of the world outside the hills.

"My ancestors were neighbors of the people of Alexander," he said at last. "So, many of my people speak their language."

They were approaching the stone roofs which shone through the trees, and Gordon saw that Bardylis's "village" was a substantial town, surrounded by a wall. It was so plainly the work of long dead Grecian architects that he felt like a man who wandered into a past and forgotten age.

Outside the walls, men tilled the thin soil with primitive implements, and herded sheep and cattle. A few horses grazed along the bank of the stream which meandered through the valley. All the men, like Bardylis, were tall and fair-haired. They dropped their work and came running up, staring at the black-haired stranger in hostile surprise, until Bardylis reassured them.

"It is the first time any but a captive or a trader has entered the valley in centuries," said Bardylis to Gordon. "Say nothing till I bid you. I wish to surprise my people with your knowledge. Zeus, they will gape when they hear a stranger speak to them in their own tongue!"

The gate in the wall hung open and unguarded, and Gordon noticed that the wall itself was in a poor state of repair. Bardylis remarked that the guard in the narrow pass at the end of the valley was sufficient protection, and that no hostile force had ever reached the city itself. They passed through and walked along a broad paved street, in which yellow-haired people in tunics, men, women and children, went about their tasks much like the Greeks of two thousand years ago, among buildings which were duplicates of the structures of ancient Athens.

A crowd quickly formed about them, but Bardylis, bursting with glee and importance, gave them no satisfaction. He went straight toward a large edifice near the center of the town and mounting the broad steps, came into a large chamber where several men, more richly dressed than the common people, sat casting dice on a small table before them. The crowd swarmed in after them, and thronged the doorway eagerly. The chiefs ceased their dice game, and one, a giant with a commanding air, demanded: "What do you wish, Bardylis? Who is this stranger?"

"A friend of Attalus, Ptolemy, king of the valley of Iskander," answered Bardylis. "He speaks the tongue of Iskander!"

"What tale is this?" harshly demanded the giant.

"Let them hear, brother!" Bardylis directed triumphantly.

"I come in peace," said Gordon briefly, in archaic Greek. "I am called El Borak, but I am no Moslem."

A murmur of surprise went up from the throng, and Ptolemy fingered his chin and scowled suspiciously. He was a magnificently built man, clean-shaven like all his tribesmen, and handsome, but his visage was moody.

He listened impatiently while Bardylis related the circumstances of his meeting with Gordon, and when he told of the American lifting the stone that pinned him down, Ptolemy frowned and involuntarily flexed his own massive thews. He seemed ill-pleased at the approval with which the people openly greeted the tale. Evidently these descendants of Grecian athletes had as much admiration for physical perfection as had their ancient ancestors, and Ptolemy was vain of his prowess.

"How could he lift such a stone?" the king broke in. "He is of no great size. His head would scarcely top my chin."

"He is mighty beyond his stature, O king," retorted Bardylis. "Here is the bruise on my leg to prove I tell the truth. He lifted the stone I could not move, and he came down the Road of the Eagles, which few even among the Altaians have dared. He has traveled far and fought men, and now he would feast and rest."

"See to it then," grunted Ptolemy contemptuously, turning back to his dice game. "If he is a Moslem spy, your head shall answer for it."

"I stake my head gladly on his honesty, O king!" answered Bardylis proudly. Then, taking Gordon's arm, he said softly, "Come my friend. Ptolemy is short of patience and scant of courtesy. Pay no heed to him. I will take you to the house of my father."

As they pushed their way through the crowd, Gordon's gaze picked out an alien countenance among the frank, blond faces—a thin, swarthy visage, whose black eyes gleamed avidly on the American. The man was a Tajik, with a bundle on his back. When he saw he was being scrutinized he smirked and bobbed his head. There was something familiar about the gesture.

"Who is that man?" Gordon asked.

"Abdullah, a Moslem dog whom we allow to enter the valley with beads and mirrors and such trinkets as our women love. We trade ore and wine and skins for them."

Gordon remembered the fellow now—a shifty character who used to hang around Peshawur, and was suspected of smuggling rifles up the Khyber Pass. But when he turned and looked back, the dark face had vanished in the crowd. However, there was no reason to fear Abdullah, even if the man recognized him. The Tajik could not know of the papers he carried. Gordon felt that the people of Attalus were friendly to the friend of Bardylis, though the youth had plainly roused Ptolemy's jealous vanity by his praise of Gordon's strength.

Bardylis conducted Gordon down the street to a large stone house with a pillared portico, where he proudly displayed his friend to his father, a venerable patriarch called Perdiccas, and his mother, a tall, stately woman, well along in years. The Attalans certainly did not keep their women in seclusion like the Moslems. Gordon saw Bradylis's sisters, robust blond beauties, and his young brother. The American could scarcely suppress a smile at the strangeness of it all, being ushered into the every-day family life of two thousand years ago. These people were definitely not barbarians. They were lower, undoubtedly, in the cultural scale than their Hellenic ancestors, but they were still more highly civilized than their fierce Afghan neighbors.

The interest in their guest was genuine, but none save Bardylis showed much interest in the world outside their valley. Presently the youth led Gordon into an inner chamber and set food and wine before him. The American ate and drank ravenously, suddenly aware of the lean days that had preceded this feast. While he ate, Bardylis talked, but he did not speak of the men who had been pursuing Gordon. Evidently he supposed them to have been Afghans of the surrounding hills, whose hostility was proverbial. Gordon learned that no man of Attalus had ever been more than a day's journey away from the valley. The ferocity of the hill tribes all about them had isolated them from the world completely.

When Gordon at last expressed a desire for sleep, Bardylis left him alone, assuring him that he would not be disturbed. The American was somewhat disturbed to find that there was no door to his chamber, merely a curtain drawn across an archway. Bardylis had said there were no thieves in Attalus, but caution was so much a natural part of Gordon that he found himself a prey to uneasiness. The room opened onto a corridor, and the corridor, he believed, gave onto an outer door. The people of Attalus apparently did not find it necessary to safeguard their dwellings. But though a native could sleep in safety, that might not apply to a stranger.

Finally Gordon drew aside the couch which formed the main piece of furniture for the chamber, and making sure no spying eyes were on him, he worked loose one of the small stone blocks which composed the wall. Taking the silk-bound packet from his shirt, he thrust it into the aperture, pushed back the stone as far as it would go, and replaced the couch.

Stretching himself, then, upon the couch, he fell to evolving plans for escape with his life and those papers which meant so much to peace of Asia. He was safe enough in the valley, but he knew Hunyadi would wait for him outside with the patience of a cobra. He could not stay here forever. He would scale the cliffs some dark night and bolt for it. Hunyadi would undoubtedly have all the tribes in the hills after him, but he would trust to luck and his good right arm, as he had so often before. The wine he had drunk was potent. Weariness after the long flight weighted his limbs. Gordon's meditations merged into dream. He slept deeply and long.

IV. THE DUEL WITH PTOLEMY THE KIND

WHEN GORDON AWOKE he was in utter darkness. He knew that he had slept for many hours, and night had fallen. Silence reigned over the house, but he had been awakened by the soft swish of the curtains over the doorway.

He sat up on his couch and asked: "Is that you, Bardylis?"

A voice grunted, "Yes." Even as he was electrified by the realization that the voice was not that of Bardylis, something crashed down on his head, and a deeper blackness, shot with fire-sparks, engulfed him.

When he regained consciousness, a torch dazzled his eyes, and in its glow he saw three men—burly, yellow-haired men of Attalus with faces more stupid and brutish than any he had yet seen. He was lying on a stone slab in a bare chamber, whose crumbling, cob-webbed walls were vaguely illumined by the guttering torch. His arms were bound, but not his legs. The sound of a door opening made him crane his neck, and he saw a stooped, vulture-like figure enter the room. It was Abdullah, the Tajik.

He looked down on the American with his rat-like features twisted in a venomous grin.

"Low lies the terrible El Borak!" he taunted. "Fool! I knew you the instant I saw you in the palace of Ptolemy."

"You have no feud with me," growled Gordon.

"A friend of mine has," answered the Tajik. "That is nothing to me, but it shall gain me profit. It is true you have never harmed me, but I have always feared you. So when I saw you in the city, I gathered my goods and hastened to depart, not knowing what you did here. But beyond the pass I met the Feringhi Hunyadi, and he asked me if I had seen you in the valley of Iskander whither you had fled to escape him. I answered that I had, and he urged me to help him steal into the valley and take from you certain documents he said you stole from him.

"But I refused, knowing that these Attalan devils would kill me if I tried to smuggle a stranger into Iskander, and Hunyadi went back into the hills with his four Turks, and the horde of ragged Afghans he has made his friends and allies. When he had gone I returned to the valley, telling the guardsmen at the pass that I feared the Pathans.

"I persuaded these three men to aid me in capturing you. None will know what became of you, and Ptolemy will not trouble himself about you, because he is jealous of your strength. It is an old tradition that the king of Attalus must be the strongest man in the city. Ptolemy would have killed you himself, in time. But I will attend to that. I do not wish to have you on my trail, after I have taken from you the

31

papers Hunyadi wishes. He shall have them ultimately—if he is willing to pay enough!" He laughed, a high, cackling laugh, and turned to the stolid Attalans. "Did you search him?"

"We found nothing," a giant rumbled.

Abdullah tck-tck'ed his teeth in annoyance.

"You do not know how to search a Feringhi. Here, I will do it myself."

He ran a practiced hand over his captive, scowling as his search was unrewarded. He tried to feel under the American's armpits, but Gordon's arms were bound so closely to his sides that this was impossible.

Abdulla frowned worriedly, and drew a curved dagger.

"Cut loose his arms," he directed, "then all three of you lay hold on him; it is like letting a leopard out of his cage."

Gordon made no resistance and was quickly spread-eagled on the slab, with a big Attalan at each arm and one on his legs. They held him closely, but seemed skeptical of Abdullah's repeated warnings concerning the stranger's strength.

The Tajik again approached his prisoner, lowering his knife as he reached out. With a dynamic release of coiled steel muscles, Gordon wrenched his legs free from the grasp of the careless Attalan and drove his heels into Abdullah's breast. Had his feet been booted they would have caved in Tajik's breast bone. As it was, the merchant shot backward with an agonized grunt, and struck the floor flat on his shoulders.

Gordon had not paused. That same terrific lunge had torn his left arm free, and heaving up on the slab, he smashed his left fist against the jaw of the man who gripped his right arm. The impact was that of a caulking hammer, and the Attalan went down like a butchered ox. The other two lunged in, hands grasping. Gordon threw himself over the slab to the floor on the other side, and as one of the warriors lunged around it, he caught the Attalan's wrist, wheeled, jerking the arm over his shoulder, and hurled the man bodily over his head. The Attalan struck the floor head-first with an impact that knocked wind and consciousness out of him together.

The remaining kidnapper was more wary. Seeing the terrible strength and blinding speed of his smaller foe, he drew a long knife and came in cautiously, seeking an opportunity for a mortal thrust. Gordon fell back, putting the slab between himself and that glimmering blade, while the other circled warily after him. Suddenly the American stooped and ripped a similar knife from the belt of the man he had first felled. As he did so, the Attalan gave a roar, cleared the slab with a lion-like bound, and slashed in mid-air at the stooping American.

Gordon crouched still lower and the gleaming blade whistled over his head. The man hit the floor feet-first, off balance, and tumbled forward, full into the knife that swept up in Gordon's hand. A strangled cry was wrung from the Attalan's lips as he felt himself impaled on the long blade, and he dragged Gordon down with him in his death struggles.

Tearing free from his weakening embrace, Gordon rose, his garments smeared with his victim's blood, the red knife in his hand. Abdullah staggered up with a croaking cry, his face green with pain. Gordon snarled like a wolf and sprang toward him, all his murderous passion fully roused. But the sight of that dripping knife and the savage mask of Gordon's face galvanized the Tajik. With a scream he sprang for the door, knocking the torch from its socket as he passed. It hit the floor, scattering sparks, and plunging the room into darkness, and Gordon caromed blindly into the wall.

When he righted himself and found the door, the room was empty except for himself and the Attalans, dead or senseless.

Emerging from the chamber, he found himself in a narrow street, with the stars fading for dawn. The building he had just quilted was dilapidated and obviously deserted. Down the narrow way he saw the house of Perdiccas. So he had not been carried far. Evidently his abductors had anticipated no interference. He wondered how much of a hand Bardylis had had in the plot. He did not like to think that the youth had betrayed him. But in any event, he would have to return to the house of Perdiccas, to obtain the packet he had concealed in the wall. He went down the street, still feeling a bit sick and giddy from that blow that had knocked him senseless, now that the fire of battle had cooled in his veins. The street was deserted. It seemed, indeed, more like an alley than a street, running between the back of the houses.

As he approached the house, he saw someone running toward him. It was Bardylis, and he threw himself on Gordon with a cry of relief that was not feigned.

"Oh, my brother!" he exclaimed. "What has happened? I found your chamber empty a short time ago, and blood on your couch. Are you unhurt? Nay, there is a cut upon your scalp!"

Gordon explained in a few words, saying nothing of the letters. He allowed Bardylis to suppose that Abdullah had been a personal enemy, bent on revenge. He trusted the youth now, but there was no need to disclose the truth of the packet.

Bardylis whitened with fury. "What a shame upon my house!" he cried. "Last night that dog Abdullah made my father a present of a great jug of wine, and we all drank except yourself, who were slumbering. I know now the wine was drugged. We slept like dogs.

"Because you were our guest, I posted a man at each outer door last night, but they fell asleep because of the wine they had drunk. A few minutes ago, searching for you, I found the servant who was posted at the door which opens

35

into this alley from the corridor that runs past your chamber. His throat had been cut. It was easy for them to creep along that corridor and into your chamber while we slept."

Back in the chamber, while Bardylis went to fetch fresh garments, Gordon retrieved the packet from the wall and stowed it under his belt. In his waking hours he preferred to keep it on his person.

Bardylis returned then with the breeches, sandals and tunic of the Attalans, and while Gordon donned them, gazed in admiration at the American's bronzed and sinewy torso, devoid as it was of the slightest trace of surplus flesh.

Gordon had scarcely completed his dressing when voices were heard without, the tramp of men resounded through the hall, and a group of yellow-haired warriors appeared at the doorway, with swords at their sides. Their leader pointed at Gordon, and said: "Ptolemy commands that this man appear at once before him, in the hall of justice."

"What is this?" exclaimed Bardylis. "El Borak is my guest!"

"It is not my part to say," answered the chief. "I but carry out the commands of our king."

Gordon laid a restraining hand on Bardylis's arm. "I will go. I want to see what business Ptolemy has with me."

"I, too, will go," said Bardylis, with a snap of his jaws. "What this portends I do not know. I do know that El Borak is my friend."

The sun was not yet rising as they strode down the white street toward the palace, but people were already moving about, and many of them followed the procession.

Mounting the broad steps of the palace, they entered a wide hall, flanked with lofty columns. At the other end there were more steps, wide and curving, leading up to a dais on which, in a throne-like marble chair, sat the king of Attalus, sullen as ever. A number of his chiefs sat on stone benches on either side of the dais, and the common people ranged themselves along the wall, leaving a wide space clear before the throne.

In this open space crouched a vulture-like figure. It was Abdullah, his eyes shining with hate and fear, and before him lay the corpse of the man Gordon had killed in the deserted house. The other two kidnappers stood nearby, their bruised features sullen and ill at ease.

Gordon was conducted into the open space before the dais, and the guards fell back on either side of him. There was little formality. Ptolemy motioned to Abdullah and said: "Make your charge."

Abdullah sprang up and pointed a skinny finger in Gordon's face.

"I accuse this man of murder!" he screeched. "This morning before dawn he attacked me and my friends while we slept, and slew him who lies there. The rest of us barely escaped with our lives!"

A mutter of surprise and anger rose from the throng. Ptolemy turned his somber stare on Gordon.

"What have you to say?"

"He lies," answered the American impatiently. "I killed that man, yes—"

He was interrupted by a fierce cry from the people, who began to surge menacingly forward, to be thrust back by the guards.

"I only defended my life," said Gordon angrily, not relishing his position of defendant. "That Tajik dog and three others, that dead man and those two standing there, slipped into my chamber last night as I slept in the house of Perdiccas, knocked me senseless and carried me away to rob and kill me."

"Aye!" cried Bardylis wrathfully. "And they slew one of my father's servants while he slept."

At that the murmur of the mob changed, and they halted in uncertainty.

"A lie!" screamed Abdullah, fired to recklessness by avarice and hate. "Bardylis is bewitched! El Borak is a wizard! How else could he speak your tongue?"

The crowd recoiled abruptly, and some made furtive signs to avert conjury. The Attalans were as superstitious as their ancestors. Bardylis had drawn his sword, and his friends rallied about him, clean-cut, rangy youngsters, quivering like hunted dogs in their eagerness.

"Wizard or man!" roared Bardylis, "he is my brother, and no man touches him save at peril of his head!"

"He is a wizard!" screamed Abdullah, foam dabbling his beard. "I know him of old! Beware of him! He will bring madness and ruin upon Attalus! On his body he bears a scroll with magic inscriptions, wherein lies his necromantic power! Give that scroll to me, and I will take it afar from Attalus and destroy it where it can do no harm. Let me prove I do not lie! Hold him while I search him, and I will show you."

"Let no man dare touch El Borak!" challenged Bardylis. Then from his throne rose Ptolemy, a great menacing image of bronze, somber and awe-inspiring. He strode down the steps, and men shrank back from his bleak eyes. Bardylis stood his ground, as if ready to defy even his terrible king, but Gordon drew the lad aside. El Borak was not one to stand quietly by while someone else defended him.

"It is true," he said without heat, "that I have a packet of papers in my garments. But it is also true that it has nothing to do with witchcraft, and that I will kill the man who tries to take it from me."

At that Ptolemy's brooding impassiveness vanished in a flame of passion.

"Will you defy even me?" he roared, his eyes blazing, his great hands working convulsively. "Do you deem yourself already king of Attalus? You black-haired dog, I will kill you with my naked hands! Back, and give us space!"

His sweeping arms hurled men right and left, and roaring like a bull, he hurled himself on Gordon. So swift and violent was his attack that Gordon was unable to avoid it. They met breast to breast, and the smaller man was hurled backward, and to his knee. Ptolemy plunged over him, unable to check his velocity, and then, locked in a death-grapple they ripped and tore, while the people surged yelling about them.

Not often did El Borak find himself opposed by a man stronger than himself. But the king of Attalus was a mass of whale-bone and iron, and nerved to blinding quickness. Neither had a weapon. It was man to man, fighting as the primitive progenitors of the race fought. There was no science about Ptolemy's onslaught. He fought like a tiger or a lion, with all the appalling frenzy of the primordial. Again and again Gordon battered his way out of a grapple that threatened to snap his spine like a rotten branch. His blinding blows ripped and smashed in a riot of destruction. The tall king of Attalus swayed and trembled before them like a tree in a storm, but always came surging back like a typhoon, lashing out with great strokes that drove Gordon staggering before him, rending and tearing with mighty fingers.

Only his desperate speed and the savage skill of boxing and wrestling that was his had saved Gordon so long. Naked to the waist, battered and bruised, his tortured body quivered with the punishment he was enduring. But Ptolemy's great chest was heaving. His face was a mask of raw beef, and his torso showed the effects of a beating that would have killed a lesser man.

Gasping a cry that was half curse, half sob, he threw himself bodily on the American, bearing him down by sheer weight. As they fell he drove a knee savagely at Gordon's groin, and tried to fall with his full weight on the smaller man's breast. A twist of his body sent the knee sliding harmlessly along his thigh, and Gordon writhed from under the heavier body as they fell.

The impact broke their holds, and they staggered up simultaneously. Through the blood and sweat that streamed into his eyes, Gordon saw the king towering above him, reeling, arms spread, blood pouring down his mighty breast. His belly went in as he drew a great laboring breath. And into the relaxed pit of his stomach Gordon, crouching, drove his left with all the strength of his rigid arm, iron shoulders and knotted calves behind it. His clenched fist sank to the wrist in Ptolemy's solar plexus. The king's breath went out of him in an explosive grunt. His hands dropped and he swayed like a tall tree under the axe. Gordon's right, hooking up in a terrible arc, met his jaw with a sound like a cooper's mallet, and Ptolemy pitched headlong and lay still.

V. THE DEATH OF HUNYADI

IN THE STUPEFIED silence that followed the fall of the king, while all eyes, dilated with surprise, were fixed on the prostrate giant and the groggy figure that weaved above him, a gasping voice shouted from outside the palace. It grew louder, mingled with a clatter of hoofs which stopped at the outer steps. All wheeled toward the door as a wild figure staggered in, spattering blood.

"A guard from the pass!" cried Bardylis.

"The Moslems!" cried the man, blood spurting through his fingers which he pressed to his shoulder. "Three hundred Afghans! They have stormed the pass! They are led by a feringhi and four turki who have rifles that fire many times without reloading! These men shot us down from afar off as we strove to defend the pass. The Afghans have entered the valley—" He swayed and fell, blood trickling from his lips. A blue bullet hole showed in his shoulder, near the base of his neck.

No clamor of terror greeted this appalling news. In the utter silence that followed, all eyes turned toward Gordon, leaning dizzily against the wall, gasping for breath.

"You have conquered Ptolemy," said Bardylis. "He is dead or senseless. While he is helpless, you are king. That is the law. Tell us what to do."

Gordon gathered his dazed wits and accepted the situation without demur or question. If the Afghans were in the valley, there was no time to waste. He thought he could hear the distant popping of firearms already. "How many men are able to bear arms?" he panted.

"Three hundred and fifty," answered one of the chiefs.

"Then let them take their weapons and follow me," he said. "The walls of the city are rotten. If we try to defend them, with Hunyadi directing the siege, we will be trapped like rats. We must win with one stroke, if at all."

Someone brought him a sheathed and belted scimitar and he buckled it about his waist. His head was still swimming and his body numb, but from some obscure reservoir he drew a fund of reserve power, and the prospect of a final showdown with Hunyadi fired his blood. At his directions men lifted Ptolemy and placed him on a couch. The king had not moved since he dropped, and Gordon thought it probable that he had a concussion of the brain. That poleax smash that had felled him would have split the skull of a lesser man.

Then Gordon remembered Abdullah, and looked about for him, but the Tajik had vanished.

At the head of the warriors of Attalus, Gordon strode down the street and through the ponderous gate. All were armed with long curved swords; some had unwieldy matchlocks, ancient weapons captured from the hill tribes.

43

He knew the Afghans would be no better armed, but the rifles of Hunyadi and his Turks would count heavily.

He could see the horde swarming up the valley, still some distance away. They were on foot. Lucky for the Attalans that one of the pass-guards had kept a horse near him. Otherwise the Afghans would have been at the very walls of the town before the word came of their invasion.

The invaders were drunk with exultation, halting to fire outlying huts and growing stuff, and to shoot cattle, in sheer wanton destructiveness. Behind Gordon rose a deep rumble of rage, and looking back at the blazing blue eyes, and tall, tense figures, the American knew he was leading no weaklings to battle.

He led them to a long straggling heap of stones which ran waveringly clear across the valley, marking an ancient fortification, long abandoned and crumbling down. It would afford some cover. When they reached it the invaders were still out of rifle fire. The Afghans had ceased their plundering and came on at an increased gait, howling like wolves.

Gordon ordered his men to lie down behind the stones, and called to him the warriors with the matchlocks—some thirty in all.

"Pay no heed to the Afghans," he instructed them. "Shoot at the men with the rifles. Do not shoot at random, but wait until I give the word, then all fire together."

The ragged horde were spreading out somewhat as they approached, loosing their matchlocks before they were in range of the grim band waiting silently along the crumbled wall. The Attalans quivered with eagerness, but Gordon gave no sign. He saw the tall, supple figure of Hunyadi, and the bulkier shapes of his turbaned Turks, in the center of the ragged crescent. The men came straight on, apparently secure in the knowledge that the Attalans had no modern weapons, and that Gordon had lost his rifle. They had seen him climbing down the cliff without it. Gordon cursed Abdullah, whose treachery had lost him his pistol.

Before they were in range of the matchlocks, Hunyadi fired, and the warrior at Gordon's side slumped over, drilled through the head. A mutter of rage and impatience ran along the line, but Gordon quieted the warriors, ordering them to lie closer behind the rocks. Hunyadi tried again, and the Turks blazed away, but the bullets whined off the stones. The men moved nearer and behind them the Afghans howled with bloodthirsty impatience, rapidly getting out of hand.

Gordon had hoped to lure Hunyadi into reach of his matchlocks. But suddenly, with an earth-shaking yell, the Afghans stormed past the Hungarian in a wave, knives flaming like the sun on water. Hunyadi yelped explosively, unable to see or shoot at his enemies, for the backs of his reckless allies. Despite his curses, they came on with a roar.

45

Gordon, crouching among the stones, glared at the gaunt giants rushing toward him until he could make out the fanatical blaze of their eyes, then he roared: "Fire."

A thunderous volley ripped out along the wall, ragged, but terrible at that range. A storm of lead blasted the oncoming line, and men went down in windrows. Lost to all caution, the Attalans leaped the wall and hewed into the staggering Afghans with naked steel. Cursing as Hunyadi had cursed, Gordon drew his scimitar and followed them.

No time for orders now, no formation, no strategy. Attalan and Afghan, they fought as men fought a thousand years ago, without order or plan, massed in a straining, grunting, hacking mob, where naked blades flickered like lightning. Yard-long Khyber knives clanged and ground against the curved swords of the Attalans. The rending of flesh and bone beneath the chopping blades was like the sound of butchers' cleavers. The dying dragged down the living and the warriors stumbled among the mangled corpses. It was a shambles where no quarter was asked and none given, and the feuds and hates of a thousand years glutted in slaughter.

No shots were fired in that deadly crush, but about the edges of the battle circled Hunyadi and the Turks, shooting with deadly accuracy. Man to man, the stalwart Attalans were a match for the hairy hillmen, and they slightly outnumbered the invaders. But they had thrown away the advantage of their position, and the rifles of the Hungarian's own party were dealing havoc in their disordered ranks. Two of the Turks were down, one hit by a matchlock ball in that first and only volley, and another disembowelled by a dying Attalan.

As Gordon hewed his way through the straining knots and flailing blades, he met one of the remaining Turks face to face. The man thrust a rifle muzzle in his face, but the hammer fell with a click on an empty shell, and the next instant Gordon's scimitar ripped through his belly and stood out a foot behind his back. As the American twisted his blade free, the other Turk fired a pistol, missed, and hurled the empty weapon fruitlessly. He rushed in, slashing with a saber at Gordon's head. El Borak parried the singing blade, and his scimitar cut the air like a blue beam, splitting the Turk's skull to the chin.

Then he saw Hunyadi. The Hungarian was groping in his belt, and Gordon knew he was out of ammunition.

"We've tried hot lead, Gustav," challenged Gordon, "and we both still live. Come and try cold steel!"

With a wild laugh the Hungarian ripped out his blade in a bright shimmer of steel that caught the morning sun. He was a tall man, Gustav Hunyadi, black sheep son of a noble Magyar house, supple and lithe as a catamount, with dancing, reckless eyes and lips that curved in a smile as cruel as a striking sword.

"I match my life against a little package of papers, El Borak!" the Hungarian laughed as the blades met.

On each side the fighting lulled and ceased, as the warriors drew back with heaving chests and dripping swords, to watch their leaders settle the score.

The curved blades sparkled in the sunlight, ground together, leaped apart, licked in and out like living things.

Well for El Borak then that his wrist was a solid mass of steel cords, that his eye was quicker and surer than a falcon's, and his brain and thews bound together with a coordination keen as razor-edged steel. For into his play Hunyadi brought all the skill of a race of swordsmen, all the craft taught by masters of the blade of Europe and Asia, and all the savage cunning he had learned in wild battles on the edges of the world.

He was taller and had the longer reach. Again and again his blade whispered at Gordon's throat. Once it touched his arm, and a trickle of crimson began. There was no sound except the rasp of feet on the sward, the rapid whisper of the blades, the deep panting of the men. Gordon was the harder pressed. That terrible fight with Ptolemy was taking its toll. His legs trembled, his sight kept blurring. As if through a mist he saw the triumphant smile growing on the thin lips of the Magyar.

And a wild surge of desperation rose in Gordon's soul, nerving him for a last rush. It came with the unexpected fury of a dying wolf, with a flaming fan of steel, a whirlwind of blades—and then Hunyadi was down, clutching at the earth with twitching hands, Gordon's narrow curved blade through him.

The Hungarian rolled his glazing eyes up at his conqueror, and his lips distorted in a ghastly smile. "To the mistress of all true adventures!" he whispered, choking on his own blood. "To the Lady Death!"

He sank back and lay still, his pallid face turned to the sky, blood oozing from his lips.

The Afghans began slinking furtively away, their morale broken, like a pack of wolves whose leader is down. Suddenly, as if waking from a dream, the Attalans gave tongue and pelted after them. The invaders broke and fled, while the infuriated Attalans followed, stabbing and hacking at their backs, down the valley and out through the pass.

Gordon was aware that Bardylis, blood-stained but exultant, was beside him, supporting his trembling frame that seemed on the point of collapse. The American wiped the bloody sweat from his eyes, and touched the packet under his girdle. Many men had died for that. But many more would have died had it not been saved, including helpless women and children.

Bardylis muttered apprehensively, and Gordon looked up to see a gigantic figure approaching leisurely from the direction of the city, through whose gate the rejoicing women were already streaming. It was Ptolemy, his features grotesquely swollen and blackened from Gordon's iron fists. He strode serenely through the heaps of corpses, and reached the spot where the companions stood.

Bardylis gripped his notched sword, and Ptolemy, seeing the gesture, grinned with his pulped lips. He was holding something behind him.

"I do not come in anger, El Borak," he said calmly. "A man who can fight as you have fought is neither wizard, thief nor murderer. I am no child to hate a man who has bested me in fair fight—and then saved my kingdom while I lay senseless. Will you take my hand?"

Gordon grasped it with an honest surge of friendship toward this giant, whose only fault, after all, was his vanity.

"I did not recover my senses in time for the battle," said Ptolemy. "I only saw the last of it. But if I did not reach the field in time to smite the Moslem dogs, I have at least rid the valley of one rat I found hiding in the palace." He casually tossed something at Gordon's feet. The severed head of Abdullah, the features frozen in a grin of horror, stared up at the American.

"Will you live in Attalus and be my brother, as well as the brother of Bardylis?" asked Ptolemy, with a glance down the valley, toward the pass through which the warriors were harrying the howling Afghans.

"I thank you, king," said Gordon, "but I must go to my own people, and it is still a long road to travel. When I have rested for a few days, I must be gone. A little food, to carry with me on my journey is all I ask from the people of Attalus, who are men as brave and valiant as their royal ancestors."